AF594825

This hook book belongs to

DUCKBILL BOOKS

USA | Canada | UK | Ireland | Australia
New Zealand | India | South Africa | China | Singapore

Duckbill Books is part of the Penguin Random House group of companies whose addresses can be found at global.penguinrandomhouse.com

Published by Penguin Random House India Pvt. Ltd
4th Floor, Capital Tower 1, MG Road,
Gurugram 122 002, Haryana, India

Penguin Random House India

First published in Duckbill Books by
Penguin Random House India 2024

10 9 8 7 6 5 4 3 2 1

ISBN 9780143463641

Typeset in Georgia by DiTech Publishing Services Pvt. Ltd
Printed at Aarvee Promotions, India

www.penguin.co.in

I WON'T WASH MY HAIR

APARNA KAPUR
illustrations by OGIN NAYAM

An imprint of Penguin Random House

‘I will not wash my hair,’ Divya said.

Her parents had gone away to Kolkata for two weeks. Alpa Masi and her dog Riksha had come to stay with her in Bagdogra.

Alpa Masi tilted her head. 'Did I give Riksha his food?' she asked.

When he heard the word 'food', Riksha jumped up and ran to the kitchen.

Divya went on. 'It is boring. Shampoo gets in my eyes. It takes so long. And it just ends up getting dirty again. I will *never* wash my—'

'Okay,' Alpa Masi said. She got up and followed Riksha.

Divya did not wash her hair for five days.

In the time she saved, she

d
u
g a h
o
l
e all the way to Chile.

At school, Ameena Ma'am made her sit at the very back of the classroom, next to the big window.

The next day, a man held his nose and said, 'Eugh! Did that dog fall asleep in a muddy puddle?'

'No, it is my hair,' Divya said.

The man crossed the road.

Ameena Ma'am made her sit outside the classroom. 'I do not want that smell in my class,' she said.

Sahil leaned out of the window and said, 'I will also stop washing my hair.' They high-fived.

At night, Divya looked at her pillow. She saw the pencil she had lost the day before, two earthworms and a chilli from Chile.

She dusted it all off and went to sleep.

Divya did not wash her hair for nine days.

In the time she saved, she learnt the language of ANTS.

'Sahil, you smell of shampoo!' Divya said.

'Sorry, Divya. I washed my hair,' Sahil said. 'My head was starting to itch.'

'So what? Scratching is a dance for your fingers.'

Ameena Ma'am made her sit in the playground.

‘One more step,’ she said through a megaphone. ‘I can still smell your hair.’

In the park, Abha would only play 'telephone'. 'Your hair worms are distracting me.'

‘I like playing telephone!’ Divya said and took her paper cup to the far end of the park.

‘The poha is really good, Alpa Masi,’ Divya said during dinner.

‘YEE! What is that?’ Alpa Masi’s eyes were wide.

‘Just some blue paint splatter from art class,’ Divya said.

But Alpa Masi leant past Divya and picked up Riksha. She pulled out a white thread stuck to Riksha's leg.

'That's better.' She smiled and started eating again.

After some time, she said, 'What's that smell?'

That night, Divya looked at her pillow. She saw a paintbrush, uncooked peanuts and an anthill.

She dusted it all off and went to sleep.

Divya did not wash her hair for thirteen days.

In the time she saved, she built a **SPACESHIP** and travelled to the edge of the universe.

Ameena Ma'am made her sit on the boundary wall.

Divya could not hear what was going on in class, but she did see a squirrel walking upside down.

On her way home, Divya walked fast. Her parents were coming back today. That meant she would get sweet potato fries again. But it also meant no Alpa Masi and no skipping hair washes.

Her parents would make her go back to having shampoo in her eyes and wasting all that time every other day. There *had* to be a way for her to avoid washing her hair.

Aparna Kapur writes and edits children's books. She once went ten days without washing her hair. In the time she saved, she drank twelve thousand cups of coffee, read ten million books, and made seven imaginary friends (because no real people wanted to be friends with her).

Ogin Nayam is a visual artist from Arunachal Pradesh. He believes his day job is to daydream. He loves working in the company of the moon and sleeps when the sun is out.

HAVALDAR HOOK WANTS SOME ANSWERS

COMPARATIVE ADJECTIVES are used to compare two people or things. SUPERLATIVE ADJECTIVES are used to compare more than two people or things. For example: Divya's hair was dirty when she didn't wash it for two days. Her hair was dirtier when she did not wash it for five days [comparative]. Her hair was the dirtiest when she didn't wash it for fourteen days [superlative].

Can you fill in the comparative and superlative forms of the adjectives below? You can select from the options on the facing page.

1 My house is big. Shalini's house is _____. But Aditi's house is the _____.

2 Rohan is tall. Rehan is _____. But Payal is the _____.

3 Billy is silly. Millie is _____. But Billu is the _____ of all.